HAIRS I[...]
OF T[...]

These two wickedly funny, wickedly realistic stories are set inside schools where chaos is the name of the game.

'Time and the Hour' takes place in a boys' school, where one class decide to conduct some research and have a bit of fun on the subject of how much time is wasted during each school day. 'Chutzpah', on the other hand, is centred in a mixed comprehensive school, where Eileen seems bent on causing as much disruption as possible on the first day of term, in the interests of democracy and women's rights.

Both stories have surprising twists at the end, but both also contain much that will be horribly familiar to anyone who has been to school!

Also published in Puffin: *Nothing to be Afraid Of*, *Thunder and Lightnings*, *Under the Autumn Garden*, *Feet and Other Stories*, and *Handles*. *The Ennead* and *Feet and Other Stories* are in Puffin Plus. *The Dead Letter Box* is in Young Puffin.

JAN MARK

HAIRS IN THE PALM
OF THE HAND

Illustrations by Stephen Lavis

PUFFIN BOOKS

Puffin Books, Penguin Books Ltd, Harmondsworth, Middlesex, England
Viking Penguin Inc., 40 West 23rd Street, New York, New York 10010, U.S.A.
Penguin Books Australia Ltd, Ringwood, Victoria, Australia
Penguin Books Canada Ltd, 2801 John Street, Markham, Ontario, Canada L3R 1B4
Penguin Books (N.Z.) Ltd, 182 190 Wairau Road, Auckland 10, New Zealand

First published by Kestrel Books 1981
Published in Puffin Books 1983
Reprinted 1984, 1985 (twice)

Printed and bound in Great Britain by
Richard Clay (The Chaucer Press) Ltd,
Bungay, Suffolk

Contents

TIME
AND THE HOUR

The door of the classroom was painted blue, with a pattern of grey fingerprints stippled round the handle. Half-way up was a nebulous blot where Mr Holland had thrown the board duster at Addison and missed, and just above that was a panel of reinforced glass behind which the Headmaster's face sometimes floated mistily, like the ghost of a drowned man come back to spy on the living.

As Martin Bennett looked up from his geometry book the glass was steamed over and a watery eye peered through. The handle turned and the door began to open with a gritty shriek as it engaged with a piece of chalk that had jammed under it.

'Well, come in,' Mr Holland yelled, from the blackboard, 'or go out, but don't stand there creating a draught, you horrible hole-and-corner merchant!'

The hole-and-corner merchant slunk in and shut the door hurriedly. It was Albone, from the second year.

'Excuse me, Sir,' said Albone. 'Sir sent me with a message, Sir.'

'Pipe down, Albone,' said Mr Holland. 'Is it a written message, Albone, or verbal?'

'It's on a piece of paper, Sir,' said Albone, who was by no means all bone, but fat, and would have sold his soul for a different name. He intended to change it as soon as he was old enough to vote.

'Small mercies,' said Mr Holland, taking the paper, limp and wrinkled from being carried round the school in Albone's hot hand. 'Lend me your ears, 1x, or to put it in the demotic, pin back your lug-holes. Here is a message from Mr Jones. All those boys who travel on the Number 11 bus please wait behind after school to see the said Mr Jones in the lower playground, as there has been a complaint. What sort of a complaint, Albone? Cholera? Trench Foot? Or a justly irate member of the public?'

'Dunno, Sir,' said Albone, shuffling. 'Sir didn't say, Sir.'

'Probably the public,' said Mr Holland. 'It's not about any of you lot, is it?' he roared, leaning across the desk, and 1x bent before the blast, hands over pinned-back lug-holes.

'Take it away, Albone,' he said. Albone retrieved his small damp document and took himself off. Mr Holland forgot about Albone and turned back to the blackboard where he wrote *Q.E.D.* underneath his fiendish tangle of triangles.

Martin consulted his watch and wrote *1 minute 15 seconds* in the little red cash book that was half concealed by the cover of his geometry folder. Mr

Holland was not always a Good Thing, on account of his temper, and his sense of humour and his smile, which was like the crack on a tombstone, but he could be depended upon to turn the most minor incident into a major disruption, and he liked to finish a lesson as soon as the bell rang. The bell was due to ring in three minutes' time and Martin was about to begin reckoning up the day's total when the door opened again and the Deputy Head walked in. He conferred with Mr Holland in low whispers and Martin eyed them, pen waiting, watch poised. He made it a rule never to time an interruption until the class was actually told to stop work, otherwise he might be tempted into malpractice, like the time the Headmaster had come in to see how a student teacher was getting on, and no one had done anything at all while he was there except watch him watching the student. But it had not been official, and at the end of the week Martin had felt honour bound to strike it from the record.

'Pay attention, *boys*,' said the Deputy Head, removing his glasses and conducting with them. He was in charge of the school orchestra. 'I expect you remember being told in assembly, several *times*, that playing cards for money is strictly *forbidden!* It appears that some *boys* imagined that they could get round this by throwing *dice* instead. I would like to point out that *any* form of gambling will be punished with the *utmost* severity.' He waved the glasses at them to stress the severity. '*Do* I make myself clear? *Thank* you, Mr Holland.'

'Thank *you*, Mr Deputy *Head*,' said Mr Holland, as the door closed behind him.

Martin wrote *45 seconds* in the cash book and drew a red line under it. The bell rang. The class began to clear up.

Martin began to add up.

As Mr Holland vanished into the corridor, Addison came wading down from the front row where he was made to sit by every member of staff in the school.

'What you up to, Benno?' he demanded, bringing his hand down flat on the cash book. 'I've been watching you. What're you doing?' Only Addison could sit in the front row and watch someone at the back.

'Get your great sweaty mauler off my work,' said Martin, shoving at it.

'No, let's have a look at it. Go on. Is it something dirty?' said Addison, unperturbed. He was a man of peace, unless he happened to be looking for a fight. Martin shrugged and let him pick up the cash book. Addison's eyes widened in disgust.

'It's adding up. It's *maths!*'

'Well, it was a maths lesson,' Martin said, reasonably.

'But you were doing it in English. And geography.

And woodwork, yesterday. I saw you. Here, you lot, look at this.' The others drew round to see what was the matter. Anything in which Addison showed an interest usually ended as a shambles. 'Benno's doing maths for *fun*. Let's kill him.'

'It's not maths,' said Martin, grabbing for the cash book. 'It's my time-wasting chart. Look here, this column where it says credit is how much time we wasted today; sixteen minutes. We were three minutes late out of assembly, see, and we lost five minutes in geography when Hopkins got his arm stuck down the radiator, and we were four minutes late getting to games because of being yelled at in the playground, and then old Barnes was two minutes late for English. We had two messages with Holland just now – that was another two minutes.'

'So what?' said Addison. 'Who cares? I don't.'

'Who cares if you care?' said Martin. 'Go and pull your head off. But look, in the debit column; we didn't start break till ten-to, because old Lever is always late finishing, and we were two minutes late out of games, finding that discus. Well, that's seven minutes saved. You take that away from sixteen and you've got nine left.'

'*Nah*. Tell me another,' said Addison. 'Hear that, Forbesy? Seven from sixteen leaves nine. They ought to give him the Nobel Prize.'

'Shut up,' said Forbes, who was looking at the

figures and hoping that Martin had slipped up somewhere: not from animosity but in a spirit of inquiry. He liked intellectual arguments and Addison's slanging bored him.

'What are you trying to prove?' said Addison. 'Einstein.'

'Well, we wasted fourteen yesterday, nine on Wednesday, twelve on Tuesday and eight on Monday. That's nearly an hour this week,' said Martin. 'Mind you, it was a good week; it's usually nearer half. I want to see if we waste a whole day by the end of term. I mean, this week's brought the total up, and we get a whole afternoon off for the inter-school sports in July. Should do it easy.'

'I bet we don't,' said Addison.

'How much?' Hopkins said, instantly.

'Let's have a kitty.' Addison's little eyes gleamed like counterfeit coins. 'We'll all put a bit in.'

'Who wins, then?' said Forbes, always practical, and naturally mistrustful of anything that Addison suggested. He had been at the junior school with Addison and Addison still owed him ten pence from the end of term raffle.

'Hang about,' said Addison, who had not forgotten the ten pence either and was still, after two terms, hoping to tempt Forbes into double or quits. 'Let's do it like they do on those cruise ships. People make bets on how far they think they'll go in a day's sailing and the one who guesses nearest wins the money. We'll all guess a time, get it? And the one who's nearest right cleans up.'

'It's months to end of term. Let's just do it for a week,' said Hopkins. 'I bet fifteen p that we waste forty-nine minutes next week.'

'Ten p on forty,' said Forbes.

'Thirty on thirty, then,' said Traill.

'Just a minute,' said Addison. 'We'll do this properly. How long have you been keeping records, Benno?'

'Four weeks – since the beginning of term,' said Martin.

'Let's have a look then,' said Addison, becoming business-like. 'Study the form. Double maths lesson's hard going.'

'They're all hard going for you,' said Forbes, under his breath.

Martin handed over the cash book, half alarmed at seeing his private survey become so suddenly public, and in Addison's hands, at that.

'Benno can make the list,' said Addison, generously, 'as it's his idea. But that means he can't bet.'

'Why not?' said Martin, bound to sound truculent, but also slightly relieved, for he had just remembered that the last interruption had been the gambling ban.

'You might fiddle it.'

'I wouldn't.'

'Look, do you want to do this properly or don't you?' said Addison, who had never before shown the slightest inclination to do anything properly. 'You'll be the official time-keeper, and Forbesy can check you out at the end of each lesson. O.K., Forbesy?' Forbes had a stop watch.

'O.K., Boss,' said Forbes, out of the side of his mouth. Addison strutted and swelled a little, like a pigeon in spring.

'You finished that list, yet, Benno?' he said. Martin had been taking down names on a sheet of file paper borrowed from Mr Holland's desk. By the time he reached the end he realized that he had listed everyone in the class except himself and Forbes. And Judd. Judd was a professional absentee. Very few people could remember what he looked like.

'There you are,' he said, finally. 'That's everyone down. Now you can fill in how much you bet, and the time you're betting on. Use your own pen,' he said, as Traill tried to take his. Traill took the pen anyway and was beginning to write *30p on 30 minutes* when Addison stayed him with a heavy hand.

'Hang on,' he said. 'I reckon we should all bet the same. That'll make it fairer.'

'But betting's *not* fair,' said Luckhurst.

'Yes, but this way's *very* not fair,' said Addison, 'I mean, someone could lay two p and clean up the lot.'

'O.K.,' said Forbes. 'We'll all bet two p.'

'Chicken feed. What's twenty-seven times two, Einstein?'

'Fifty-four pence,' said Martin.

'You mean we should go through all this – ' he made it sound like an assault course ' – for fifty-four measly pence? I was going to lay a pound.'

'A *pound?*'

'A oncer,' said Flash Addison, and matched word with deed by laying a pound note on the desk. It fluttered a little as they all breathed enviously upon it. 'Right, gentlemen. Let's see the colour of your money.'

'I haven't got a pound,' said Hopkins 'I bet fifteen, and fifteen's what I got.'

'Make it fifty,' said Addison.

'I've only got *fifteen.*'

'You'll have fifty by next week though, won't you?' said Addison. 'I mean, we all get pocket money, don't we? And it's safer this way. You know what they said about gambling. So long as we know what times we're betting on, we needn't pay up till next week. That'll give Hoppo a chance to save up his fifty, and no cash changes hands, so they can't do us for that. Whoever wins can collect after school, or something. Sixteen hundred hours sharp, next Friday, at the 125 bus stop. None of the teachers catch the 125.'

'Fifty's a heck of a lot,' said Traill.

'Ah, but think what you might win,' said Addison, whipping away his oncer at high speed. 'Now, write down the times, quick. Go on, Traill. You've got the pen.'

'What about if it comes out even?' said Forbes. 'I mean, supposing we save as much as we waste?'

'Nobody wins,' said Addison. 'It never comes out the other way, does it, Benno? We never end up saving more time, do we?'

'Not so far.'

'Right, then,' said Addison, seeing that everyone else had finished. 'I bet we *save* fifteen minutes next week.'

'Save it?' said Martin. 'But we never...'

'Live dangerously,' said Addison.

'Do you know something we don't?' Hopkins said, suspiciously.

'I like long odds. Anybody want to chicken out?' said Addison. Nobody did. In the background someone muttered, 'You could pick up thirteen quid on this, not counting your own stake.'

Mr Jones looked in at the door, scowling and hairy in his games kit and fresh from savaging the travellers from the Number 11 bus.

'What are you doing in here then? If you're not outside in thirty seconds I'll keep you in for thirty minutes, Monday lunch time.'

That would be half an hour to Addison before they had even started. They scattered, Martin too, with a final glance at his betting slip. There was £13.50 at stake, and it was Addison's doing.

What was he up to?

2

Monday began very promisingly, with a long assembly that chewed ten minutes out of Mr Lever's geography lesson. Martin and Forbes smiled at each other across the room and raised their synchronized watches in a secret toast. But Mr Lever, as Martin had pointed out, was always late finishing, and he was followed by Mr Allard who taught physics in a laboratory full of fragile equipment, where Addison frisked like a bull in a china shop. Martin would have thought that anyone who was made to sit in the front row ought to have more sense than to construct a siege engine out of a rubber newt and a perspex ruler that snapped in half when Addison fired it. Addison released his newt just as Mr Allard was giving the order to clear away apparatus, and by the time the glass had been swept up the ten minutes had been reduced to five.

Then Traill asked a silly question in history and Mr Gates kindly allowed them all to remain behind for two minutes after the bell, while he answered it. Martin had a nasty thought, then, and could only hope that it wouldn't occur to Addison. If enough silly questions were asked at the end of enough lessons, precious moments might be saved, and his suspicions mounted when Addison asked a superbly silly question in the French class. He actually asked it in French, and the teacher was so delighted to be asked anything at all by Addison, apart from 'Can I be excused, Sir?' that he answered it in French, while the class squirmed and looked pointedly at the clock over the door. Forbes became distraught, and raised his hand.

'Monsieur, regardez-vous l'horloge, s'il vous plait?'

'Belt up, Forbes,' said the French master, ungratefully.

Someone might have said something to Addison at afternoon break, but he had pressing appointments with at least two members of staff and did not reappear until the beginning of the arithmetic lesson. Half-way through, in came Albone with one of his bits of paper.

'Another moist message,' said Mr Holland, taking it. 'Pin back, etcetera, 1x. This means you. The Headmaster has noticed a tendency to fight – only a tendency, mind you – on the main staircase, due to certain boys trying to ascend and descend on the same side. In future, he says, you will kindly go up on the right and down on the left. That's all. Thank you, Albone. Remove it.'

Martin was about to write *30 seconds* when Hopkins put up his hand.

'Sir! He doesn't really mean that, does he, Sir?'

'I imagine he does, Hopkins. Perhaps you would like to go and tell our Headmaster that he doesn't know what he's talking about?'

'But Sir, if you go up on the right you have to come down on the right too, Sir, otherwise you'd run into yourself going the other way, wouldn't you, Sir?'

'Explain yourself, Hopkins. This sounds like physics to me.'

'Well, Sir, if you go upstairs on the right, like this – ' Hopkins left his seat and advanced upon Mr Holland, highstepping to indicate going upstairs, ' – and then turn round, Sir, the side you came up on is the left, and the side you *didn't* come up on is the right. So – ' Hopkins turned round, knees at full throttle, and went back again, ' – you have to go down on the right, too, because the left side *is* the right side, if you're coming up.' Hopkins turned smartly on one foot and fell over. 'It won't work, Sir,' he said plaintively, from under the desk, in the voice of one who has suffered on behalf of logical thought.

'I believe you have convinced me, Hopkins,' said Mr Holland. 'I look forward to seeing what happens at the end of the afternoon when theory becomes practice, and I certainly shall be there to watch,' he added, threateningly, 'so take my advice, 1x, and stay on the ground floor.'

Martin glanced at Forbes. Forbes raised five fingers, then seven, and waggled them slightly. Martin wrote *5 minutes 7 seconds!!!!!* The arithmetic lesson occupied a double period with Mr Holland, so unless Addison managed to out-Hopkins Hopkins at four o'clock, they should get away on time. Sure enough, as the bell rang, Addison was ready with his silly question.

'Sir? Why is an obtuse angle called an obtuse angle?'

'Because it's thick, Addison, like you,' said Mr Holland, fingers on the door handle. Addison did not give up so easily.

'But Sir, why's an acute angle called an acute angle...?'

'Addison, I don't give a damn, and neither do you. Good afternoon,' said Mr Holland, and was out of the room before the bell stopped ringing.

They had more than seven minutes in hand.

Tuesday's assembly was also long, owing to the Headmaster's explaining in detail what happened when people blindly obeyed orders instead of thinking for themselves. He recited poetry.

> '"*Forward, the Light Brigade!*"
> *Was there a man dismay'd?*
> *Not though the soldier knew*
> *   Someone had blunder'd:*
> *Theirs not to make reply,*
> *Theirs not to reason why,*
> *Theirs but to do and die:*
> *Into the valley of Death*
> *   Rode the six hundred.*'

'And you know what happened to *them*,' said the Headmaster. 'Blown to bits.'

It was only gradually that anyone realized he was talking about going upstairs on the right and coming down on the left. Hopkins capered and shook hands with himself like a victorious boxer, and was ordered outside by Mr Holland who threw a packet of Rothmans at him and was unchivalrous enough to demand them back, afterwards.

This gave them an eight-minute start, but it was whittled away during the day by Addison, asking questions like a quizmaster at the end of each lesson. His new thirst for knowledge was meeting with approval among the more innocent members of staff, and it was only Mr Holland who told him to shut up in case he learned something by accident and had to be put to bed to recover. Mr Holland was deputizing for an absent teacher, and marking homework at the same time, which was hard luck on Addison. It was 1x's homework.

'Talking of learning, Addison,' said Mr Holland, 'isn't it time you learned to write?'

'I can write, Sir,' said Addison, waving his pen to prove that he was at least equipped to try, and ejecting an air-to-air missile of ink that caught Traill right between the eyes.

'I only mentioned it,' said Mr Holland, 'because I happen to have your arithmetic homework lying open before me, at this very moment, on the desk. Did you write it with your feet, by any chance?'

'With my hand, Sir,' said Addison.

'Well try using your feet next time,' said Mr Holland. 'You might get a better grip on the pen. No, don't bother to protest, Addison. The bell is about to ring and I should hate to detain you all. Get along to Mr Allard.'

Martin put away the cash book, untouched, and got along with the others to Mr Allard, in the laboratory. If Mr Allard ran true to form they would be left with even less time, but they were saved by Forbes who managed to trap Mr Allard into talking about his army service in Malaya, for a whole ten minutes. They knew from past experience that Mr Allard preferred Malaya to chemistry.

'Malaya was a piece of cake compared with you lot,' said Mr Allard, and spoke happily of the good old days when the heat was enough to strike you down dead, and guerillas lurked in the jungle, and Addison hadn't even been thought of.

'I had been thought of,' said Addison, offended.

'I refuse to believe you were planned in advance, Addison,' said Mr Allard. 'If so, you were a tactical error. Open your books.'

'Now here's a curious thing,' said Mr Gates, burrowing like a dachshund after badgers in the bottom of the stock cupboard. 'No chalk. Not a stick, not a stub, not a stiver. Who's the chalk monitor in this outfit?'

'Me, Sir,' said Luckhurst.

'So where's the chalk, Luckhurst?'

'We had half a box full last week,' said Luckhurst. I remember, because we lent some to Mr Lever.'

'There's none there now. You'd better go and borrow some back. Hurry up.'

Luckhurst went out obliquely, knocking against desks and tripping over duffle bags to give the impression of frantic haste while at the same time moving very slowly. Mr Gates was new and gullible, but not *that* gullible.

'Try shutting your head in the door,' he advised. 'Much more convincing. Right, the rest of you can finish reading the chapter.'

Hopkins put up his hand.

'Sir, what's the difference between a thing being half empty and being half full?'

'Depends how full you want it to be,' said Mr Gates. 'If it's a bottle of whisky, it's half full. If it's a bottle of flat beer, it's half empty.'

'Wo-ho-ho!' said everyone, at the mention of strong drink.

'What's a box of chalk, then?' said a voice at the back.

'That depends on how badly you want the chalk,' said Mr Gates. Luckhurst put his head round the door.

'Mr Lever hasn't got any, either. He was just sending someone down to us, Sir, to borrow a bit.'

'Well, go and ask elsewhere, Luckhurst. Use the famous brain.'

'It's not me that's got a famous brain,' said Luckhurst.

'Nor it is. Well, use whatever you've got instead and find me some chalk,' said Mr Gates. 'We've wasted five minutes already.'

'Four minutes and nineteen seconds,' said Forbes, without thinking.

'Really? Are you timing me, Forbes?'

'Just happened to look at my watch, Sir,' said Forbes, who hadn't taken his eyes off it since the lesson began. The four minutes and nineteen seconds had stretched to six minutes and two seconds before Luckhurst returned with three centimetres of pink pastel crayon, borrowed from the Art Room.

'Very pretty,' said Mr Gates. 'Is this really the best you could come up with?'

'Yes, Sir,' said Luckhurst, and they all knew he was telling the truth because he was obviously losing his temper. 'Nobody's got any chalk at all on this corridor. They're all running up and down borrowing bits off each other. And Mr Whiteman says if anyone else comes down the Art Room for chalk he'll stuff it up their nose, Sir.'

Nothing more was said about chalk until afternoon registration, when 1x were confronted by Mr Holland, snarling behind the register.

'Addison, Ainsley, Beale, Beddows, Bennett, Chapman, Crow, Forbes, Hopkins – yes, Hopkins. Your jacket is covered in chalk dust, Hopkins. What have you been doing?'

'I must have leaned on the board, Sir,' said Hopkins, wide-eyed.

'Must you, Hopkins? The fact that you are covered in chalk dust would have nothing to do with the fact that seven classrooms found themselves without chalk, this morning, after break? Ours included? Eh, Hopkins?'

'No, Sir,' said Hopkins, unblushingly. '*We've* got chalk, Sir. In the drawer of your desk, Sir.'

'Mr Gates says there was no chalk there this morning,' said Mr Holland. 'And none in the stock cupboard.'

'*He* couldn't find any,' murmured Traill.

'Nor could anyone else,' said Mr Holland. 'Hopkins, if you are playing silly games again, I advise you to think twice. I'm watching you. Right? We aren't going to run out of file paper, are we? There's a new packet here, *and I've seen it*. Now; Hughes, Jackson, Jefferson, Johnson, Judd... Has anyone caught a glimpse of Judd this term?'

'Perhaps he's dead,' said Forbes, helpfully. They were only half through the register and the bell was due to ring in seven seconds.

'I don't think he is, Forbes. Just giving a passable imitation. He's not too dead to go fishing on Saturdays, I hear. Luckhurst, Lynch, Mankelow...'

'Listen, Hoppo,' Martin hissed, under cover of his biology folder, 'the worse you get, the worse Addison gets. You don't *need* to fiddle things. We always waste more time than we save. He can't win.'

'You tell him that,' Hopkins muttered. 'Anyway, I'm doing it for all of us, not just me.'

'Saint Hoppo,' Forbes jeered, from the other side of the bench. 'You're doing it 'cause you like doing it. Addison'll go spare if you muck up any more lessons. He'll do something horrible and then we'll all cop it. We nearly copped it this morning and that was your fault, not his.'

'Stop nattering, boys,' said Mr Jones, in his musical Welsh voice, 'or I'll bang your bloody heads together.'

'*You didn't have to pinch everybody's chalk, did you?*' Martin wrote it on a piece of paper and pushed it along to Hopkins.

'*It would of been 4m 19s not 6m 27s if i hadn't of,*' Hopkins replied.

Martin wrote, '*What about the Fehling's solution?*' and passed it over.

'What are you doing, Bennett?' said Mr Jones.

'Just doodling, Sir. Sorry, Sir,' Martin said, very politely. Mr Jones was quiet and relatively courteous in the laboratory, but a madman on the football field, and they could never be sure that he wouldn't break out spectacularly in the middle of a biology lesson, hurling himself full length down a bench full of apparatus, or practising drop kicks with the pickled rabbit.

'Confine your doodling to the diagram, please, Bennett,' said Mr Jones. He was becoming confused because people kept asking him questions, even inquiring after the health of Mrs Jones and the twins. 1x had the vague idea that Mr Jones had managed to produce twins because he taught biology. No one else on the staff had twins. Most of them hadn't even got as far as marrying.

'Addison, leave that bladder alone or I'll pull your arm off and hit you with the wet end.'

'I was just wondering if you could do osmosis with spit, Sir,' said Addison.

'*Did* you spit in it?' said Mr Jones, advancing upon Addison with menace in his Celtic eye.

'It's all talk with him,' said Hopkins. 'He's always threatening to pull our arms off or kick our heads in, but he never does. He said he'd have my ears for egg-cosies once.'

'He'll end up in the nut-house,' said Forbes. 'It's not good for him, bottling it all up He'll go mad one day and tear someone in half.'

'Watch his hands,' said Hopkins. 'The second sign of madness is hairs growing in the palm of the hand.'

'What's the first sign, then?' said Forbes, inspecting a grey palm, innocent of whiskers.

'Looking for them,' said Hopkins, smirking.

'If he tears anyone in half it ought to be you,' Forbes said, sourly. 'In fact, it probably will be you.'

'Homework!' sang Mr Jones, observing happily that it was almost four o'clock. 'I want you to finish the diagram – assuming that you've started it, and answer numbers seven to sixteen on page 93. Any questions?' he said, without thinking. Addison's hand went up. Fool, said Mr Jones, to himself.

'Why can't we do one to six as well, Sir? I'd *like* to do one to six,' said Addison, virtuously.

'I dare say, but I don't want to mark one to six,' said Mr Jones. 'Homework to be handed in on Friday morning as usual, please. Books away. There goes the bell. Line up.'

Addison closed in again.

'Sir, what is an ovary?'

'A *what?*'

'An ovary, Sir. I just happened to see the word in the index as I was shutting my book.'

'It's got nothing to do with osmosis,' said Mr Jones, feverishly. 'And you can look it up in any dictionary.' His bus went at five past four.

'I thought perhaps it was something to do with cricket,' said Addison. 'So I wondered why it was in a biology book. You know, Sir. The Oval. Where they play cricket, Sir. And overs... *maiden* overs,' he said, inspired to further excesses.

Mr Jones was trapped. He simply could not help answering questions, even though the next bus did not leave until ten to five. 'The Oval's called the Oval because it's egg-shaped. Ovum is the Latin word for egg. Line up, Addison.'

'But what's an ovary?' Addison persisted. Martin and Forbes exchanged glum glances across their watches.

'It's where eggs are produced,' said Mr Jones.

'Aha!' cried Addison. 'Battery hens!' Hopkins decided to intervene.

'I'll tell him, Sir,' he said, with a fearful wink at the hapless Jones. 'I'll make him understand,' he added, and wrung an imaginary neck.

'Thank you, Hopkins. Leave the room, boys,' said Mr Jones, taking care to be first out of the door.

'Foiled again,' said Hopkins to Addison, as they all surged after him.

'Who dropped that bottle of Fehling's solution, then?' Addison snapped. 'I suppose that was an accident, I don't think.'

Martin retired to the cycle shed with Forbes, to compare notes.

'D'you reckon Hoppo dropped that bottle on purpose?' Forbes said.

'No. If he did, he's a nutter. It didn't waste our

time, except when we all jumped. That only took three seconds. You can't count three seconds. He was the one who had to clear it up,' said Martin.

'What's the score, so far?'

'Twenty-one lost today, which isn't bad – in fact it's fantastic – but eleven saved. That's terrible. Perhaps we better had count the three seconds.'

'Addison and his silly questions. Trouble is, those questions, they only take a minute or two each, but when you add them all up...'

'I didn't think he'd try to nobble the staff,' Martin said, bitterly. 'Please Sir, yes Sir, no Sir, thank you Sir, three bags full Sir. Makes you want to puke. Someone should nobble him – with a brick.'

'Hoppo *almost* makes up for him,' said Forbes. 'But he's so obvious. Old Holland's on to him already, if you ask me. What's the total, so far?'

'Twenty-three wasted, all told,' said Martin 'That's about average for Wednesday evening, but the figures don't show what's really happening. I mean, everyone's wasting more time, because of Hoppo, but then we're saving more time because of Addison.'

'Who's winning?'

'Not either of them,' said Martin. 'Hoppo bet on wasting forty-nine minutes – look. He's never going to make that unless he kills a teacher, or something.'

'Yes, but Addison bet we'd *save* fifteen I'll tell you something, Benno. He's got a plan.'

'That's what I thought,' said Martin. 'But if him

and Hoppo go on like this it's going to come out even and no one will win.'

'That might be just as well,' Forbes said, slowly. 'The ones who bet we wouldn't save much are backing up Addison, and the ones who bet high are backing up Hoppo. Hoppo says he's doing it for all our sakes, but Addison's just doing it for Addison. I tell you, he knows he's going to win.'

'Can you imagine what it's going to be like by Friday?' said Martin, deeply depressed. 'All the lessons'll start half an hour late and never end.'

'I'm going to set fire to the school,' said Forbes.

'Don't bother. The rest of the class'll set fire to us,' said Martin. 'Especially me. I started it.'

'I'll come and put you out,' Forbes said, comfortingly. Martin smiled a thin smile. At least he had found a friend.

3

On Thursday they learned about stalactites and stalagmites, but in spite of Hopkins's best endeavours they had found out how to tell the difference by the end of the lesson.

'Stalactites come down from the ceiling,' said Mr Lever, 'and stalagmites grow up from the ground.'

'Is that where you get prisoner-of-war camps from?' Addison asked in perfect time with the first note of the bell.

'No it isn't!' the entire class yelled back.

'Well, *you* know, Sir,' said Addison, confidingly. 'Stalag Luft and Stalag Mite...'

'Ingenious but inaccurate,' said Mr Lever. 'Bring your dictionary here, Addison, and I'll explain. The rest of you can go.'

'How does it feel to cut your own throat?' Hopkins asked gleefully, as he went out.

'Let's make stacolites,' said Traill, at lunch time.

'Stalactites,' said Luckhurst. 'What d'you mean, make them? They take millions of years or something, Sir said.'

'Not this kind,' said Traill, and he told Luckhurst exactly how to make stalactites in a matter of minutes. Traill and Luckhurst and one or two others spent the lunch hour producing papier mâché.

'I thought you said minutes,' said Luckhurst, after discovering just how long it took to reduce a sheet of file paper to pulp by chewing it. Traill, meanwhile, produced a pocket full of long curly shavings from the woodwork class and wound them into tight cylinders which were embedded in the balls of pulp. They occupied the remaining few minutes of the lunch hour by tossing the balls up to the ceiling where they flattened out and stuck. Martin and Forbes came in while they were doing it.

''Ullo, 'ullo, 'ullo, wot's all this then,' said Forbes, only half joking. 'Whose head are they going to come down on? We aren't in here, first period.'

'No, fifth year, with old Barnes,' said Luckhurst.

'Anyway, they don't come down, do they, Traill?' He sniggered.

'Not all the way down,' said Traill, also sniggering. 'It's the wood shavings, see, Forbesy. They unwind.'

'They're stalactites,' said Luckhurst. 'As the paper dries out, the stalactites come down. Just as old Barnes gets going on his Shakespeare. To be or not to be, twiddly-widdly, down they come. *Un*twiddly-widdly,' he corrected himself.

'You off your head?' Forbes asked, incredulously. 'You gone bananas? You know what'll happen when Barnes sees that lot coming down? He'll know who put them there.'

'So what? I just wish we could be here to see. Maybe I could get sent with a message...'

'Who told you how to do that?' said Martin, watching damp patches spread round the stalactites.

'Traill,' said Luckhurst. 'Didn't you, Traill?'

'Oh, did you?' said Forbes. 'And what do you think old Barnes'll do? Stand there and count them? He'll have your guts for garters, that's what, Traill.'

'Who's snitching on me, then?' Traill demanded. 'You and whose army?'

'No one'll snitch,' said Martin. 'Don't you see? Sir'll say "Who did this?" and no one will tell him, and we'll all get kept in to clean up and do detention. Wilful damage to school property, and all that. Grow up, Traill. You're playing straight into Addison's hands.'

'Oh,' said Traill, and went very quiet.

'Well, thickhead?'

'It was Addison who told me how to make them,' said Traill.

Forbes flung himself down and banged his head on the desk. 'I bet it was,' he moaned, drumming with his fists on the lid. 'I bet it was. You're worse than Hoppo, you are. Barmy... bat-brain... nit-wit... dried-up *onion*...' Words failed him.

'If I was you,' said Martin, absent-mindedly patting Forbes on the head, 'I'd get something sharp and poke them down. Now. You've got about three minutes before the bell.'

'And you can poke Addison too,' said Traill, as Luckhurst dived for the window pole. 'Right in one ear and out the other.'

'Good thing Hoppo never saw,' said Forbes. 'He'd probably pinch the blackboard this time, to make up for it.'

The stalactites were removed before Mr Holland arrived for afternoon registration. Unfortunately, when he did arrive, they were being stuffed down the back of Addison's neck. Luckhurst was helping them on their way with the window pole. Mr Holland suggested mildly, since he knew no one would refuse, that they might like to stay in at break and consider their sins, including wanton wastage of file paper.

'If you'd swallowed it, Traill, to eke out your miserable portion of school dinner, I could understand it,' he said. 'But to use it for poulticing Addison comes under the heading of Useless Pastimes. Come back here at break please, all of you. Yes, I know it's unfair, but I'm feeling unfair today. If it's any consolation, you can consider this a by-product of the Great Chalk Robbery, which I have not forgotten, Hopkins. Don't anyone make me feel more unfair by forgetting to turn up. Right, Addison, Ainsley, Beale, Beddows, Bennett ...'

'Could be worse,' whispered Forbes. 'If those stalactites had stayed there he'd have kept us in after school, or something. How's the list?'

'Dodgy,' said Martin. Just how dodgy they discovered at the end of the afternoon. The unthinkable had happened. They had wasted eight minutes and saved fifteen. The total for the whole week stood at sixteen minutes wasted. One day left, and there was Addison's trump card to come, they were sure of that.

Back in September, before he came to know Hopkins properly, Mr Holland had made Hopkins responsible for collecting homework. As the class prepared to go to assembly, Hopkins gathered the two piles of exercise books, French and biology, and staggered upstairs to put them on the shelf outside the Staff Room. Just after the English lesson began, miraculously on time, Mr Jones put his head round the door.

'Excuse me,' he said, diffidently. 'May I take a moment of your time, Mr Barnes?' Martin glanced at Forbes and looked at his watch. 'I don't seem to be able to find 1x's biology homework. Does anyone know where it is?'

No one knew.

'Well, who took it up to the Staff Room?' said Mr Barnes.

'I did, Sir,' said Hopkins, rising. 'I took it up just before assembly.'

'It's not there now,' said Mr Jones.

'Go and look,' said Mr Barnes.

'Perhaps one of the other teachers took it by mistake, Sir?' said Traill.

'I have asked,' said Mr Jones. 'In any case, who'd take your biology homework if he didn't have to?'

'Get on with it, Hopkins,' said Mr Barnes.

Hopkins went to look and came back empty-handed. 'It's not there, Sir.'

'I know it's not there. Where is it?' said Mr Jones, and they saw the footballer begin to take over the biologist, as Mr Hyde took over Dr Jekyll, but Hopkins stood his ground and the wasted score had crept up to twenty-one minutes before Mr Jones retired, defeated.

However, as the bell rang for break, he was back again.

'I have searched thoroughly,' he said, in a dangerous little voice. 'I have not found. Nobody leaves this room until someone – ' he looked at Hopkins ' – remembers where those books have gone.' He blocked the doorway.

1x sat in silence, wondering how long Hopkins's amnesia would last. The score had slid down to sixteen again, before Hopkins cracked.

'I've just remembered, Sir,' he said, in broken tones. 'I had to come back to fetch my hymn book, Sir, out of my desk. I must have – have – '

'Must have?' said Mr Jones, encouragingly.

'Must have left them in my desk, Sir,' said Hopkins. He opened the lid and the twenty-nine biology books, plus twenty-nine French books, squashed down by the weight of his guilty hands, sprung up, quivering.

'You do not have a head like a sieve, boyo,' said Mr Jones, through his teeth. 'You have a spongy receptacle filled with unidentified waste matter.' He gave the spongy receptacle a parting clout with the pile of books, and was about to leave when he paused at the door.

'Since it is raining, and not likely to stop, there will be no athletics practice after break. Basketball in the gym, instead, and you had better go and get changed *now* because if any one of you is so much as one second late I shall keep you *all* in at lunch time to make up for it.'

He went. The score was down to thirteen.

They went; roughing-up Hopkins on the way to the changing room.

'What you go and do that for?' Traill yelled at him. 'You know you can't possibly win now.'

'I did it for Luckhurst,' said Hopkins. 'He bet seventeen, remember? I nearly pulled it off, too, only old Jonesy came back too soon. I was going to take the books back at break.'

'Then thanks for nothing,' said Luckhurst. 'D'you think Addison's given up yet, you horrible lurgey?'

'Nice to know who your friends are,' said Hopkins.

By the end of break everyone had changed into kit, but by the beginning of the games period, no one was waiting in the gym. On the way over, Addison was observed to wander forgetfully in the wrong direction. Several people rushed to help him recall his destination, in case he should fail to arrive on time, with the result that not only Addison but the entire class was late.

'I warned you,' said Mr Jones, 'and I meant it. You've wasted enough of my time today, between you. Report to my room at one o'clock, all of you. Traill, Forbes, pick sides.'

Friday afternoon was unspeakable in any week. It began with a double period of algebra, followed by a double period of geometry, so that the class was in Mr Holland's company for the whole afternoon. This time they had to sit there in the knowledge that Mr Jones's detention had put the score at seventeen minutes saved, only two minutes over Addison's estimate.

Addison had won. There was no chance of losing seventeen minutes, even with Mr Holland around, unless Forbes carried out his threat and set fire to the school. Mr Holland had compiled a little test to cheer them all up, he said, with his awful smile. 'Lovely, lovely maths,' he said, handing out file paper. 'And lovely, lovely file paper to do it on. One piece for you Hopkins; one for Forbes, one for Traill – don't eat it all at once, Traill.'

'Sadist,' muttered Traill. 'Aaaaaargh!'

'Oh dear, did I jog your poor head with my elbow, Traill? So sorry.' Mr Holland went back to the front of the room and sat down at his desk. Albone came in with a message.

'No need to stop work, boys,' said Mr Holland. 'I'll *memorize* it, and tell you all about it when you've finished. Take it away, Albone.'

Martin finished early and put his answer paper on one side so that he could concentrate on the more urgent problem; those lists of all the minutes lost and gained during the previous week. He checked and rechecked, but there was no way he could make a different total on either side. There, in cold ink, was the proof that 1x had actually saved seventeen minutes of working time, and that Addison was getting ready to collect £13 at the 125 bus stop, at four o'clock.

When the first period ended Mr Holland called a halt and collected the test papers.

'Sir, what was the message, Sir?' said Hopkins, hoping for a nice long one.

'No orchestra practice on Monday,' said Mr Holland. 'Hardly worth waiting for, was it, Hopkins?' He turned to demonstrate fresh miseries upon the blackboard.

Martin felt that it would be sensible to look tremendously interested, so the lesson was nearly over before he realized what he had done. The test paper was still on his desk. He had handed in the time-wasting list and it was sitting there, under Mr Holland's nose. Martin felt as though he had been punched in the stomach, drowned in freezing water, lightly boiled and spun dry in a turbine. Not only did the paper show all the time saved and wasted, the reverse side bore a list of every boy's name in the class, except his own, and Forbes's and Judd's; alongside the number of minutes they had bet on.

Evidence. Exhibit A.

At the end of the lesson, undelayed by silly questions, he approached the teacher's desk.

'Sir?'

'Bennett?'

'I think I handed in the wrong paper, Sir.'

'I think you did, Bennett. I was just reading it,' said Mr Holland. 'Would you care to explain?'

'Sir?' Martin looked round sickly at the rest of the class filing out; Addison strutting, Hopkins pale green.

'I thought not. Well then, let me guess. This is an

interesting document. If I interpret it aright, you are keeping a record of all the minutes wasted during the school week. Very public-spirited of you. It's called time and motion study. Are you going to show the Head?'

'Just doing it for fun, Sir,' Martin mumbled.

'No doubt. The second column appears to show that a certain amount of time is made up by procrastinating teachers who fail to stop when the bell rings, or who keep whole classes in because one sinful soul won't own up.'

'Procrastinating?' It said nothing on the chart about how the time was saved. Martin began to wonder about Mr Holland.

'Look it up. I suppose all this has nothing to do with Forbes telling Luckhurst that he can keep Mr Allard talking about Malaya *ad infinitum* – you can look that up, too – at the end of chemistry, last Tuesday?'

'No, Sir.'

'Of course not. So the fact that Mr Jones was obliged to spend half the morning looking for your homework has nothing to do with the fact that he had also to keep you in at lunch time?'

'No.'

'Good. I should hate to think we were being used. Teachers do talk to each other in the Staff Room you know, Bennett, and we compare notes, on occasion. We have been comparing notes. One might almost suppose that there was money at stake.'

'Sir?'

'Good again. You know what the Deputy Head said about gambling. But let us suppose that there *was* money at stake, a little flutter between gentlemen, say; Addison, who does rather tend to chuck his money around, would be in a position to wager more than the rest of you, wouldn't he?'

'Yes, Sir.' Why deny it? Addison's dad was East Kent Electronics Ltd.

'Whereupon the rest of you would be shamed into raising your stakes. Mmm. I'm not a complete idiot, Bennett. Nor am I deaf. Mr Allard is not deaf. Now, let us suppose farther that certain persons bet on a certain amount of time being wasted, but that Addison bet on a great deal of time being saved; it would be in his interest to get the class kept in. Yes? Hopkins, on the other hand, seems to have bet the other way, which may account for his having lost several pounds of chalk on Wednesday and fifty-eight exercise books this morning. What happens if you break even?'

'Nobody wins, Sir.'

'I see.' Mr Holland frowned at the list. 'And has any money changed hands?'

'No, Sir,' said Martin, glad to be able to tell the whole truth for once.

'Perish the thought. So at this particular moment, and I ask only out of curiosity, Bennett, seventeen minutes stand between a certain winner and his winnings?'

'Yes, Sir.'

'*Winnings*, Bennett?'

'Well, just knowing that he was right, Sir.'

'Let's stop this nonsense, Bennett. Obviously I can't ask you to grass on the others, but how much did you stake, personally?'

'I didn't, Sir. I'm the bookmaker.'

'You're a rotten bookmaker, Bennett. You should study the tic-tac men and never write anything down. Well, only an Act of God can save you now, Bennett; earthquake or lightning or the school catching...'

'Sir?'

'Oh, go away, you depressing youth. I'll see you later.' He went stumping off to the Staff Room with the test papers in his pocket and the time-wasting chart in his hand.

4

Martin found Forbes lurking outside.

'I never meant to tell – '

'You didn't tell,' said Forbes. 'I heard it all. It was Third Degree.'

'But you know what I went and did.'

'Oh, the wrong paper. Didn't make any difference, did it? Just confirmed his suspicions. He knew what was going on, they all did. Can't you just see them in that Staff Room, yak, yak, yak. What's he going to do?'

'I don't know. Come on, let's get outside before we're chucked out,' said Martin. 'He should have stopped it earlier.'

'I bet he's enjoying it. He ought- to stop it now. Hey!' Forbes paused. 'Does he know about the £13.50?'

'It wasn't on the paper.'

Forbes went through the motions of fainting with relief. 'Don't let's go outside,' he said urgently. 'They're doing Hoppo over, round behind the kitchen. I don't want to get involved.'

'Why don't they do Addison over?'

'Half of them were helping him,' said Forbes, ''till they realized he was winning.'

'The other half were helping Hoppo. They're doing him over, all right.'

'No one ever does Addison over,' said Forbes. '*Why* don't they? Let's hang about in the cloakroom until the bell goes.'

They slid into the cloakroom and arranged themselves alongside a row of coats, trying to look as if they were hanging up, in case a teacher happened by. Forbes actually eased a hook under his collar and dangled with limp arms and buckled knees.

'At this rate we'll all have hairs in the palm of the

hand,' said Martin, shifting his head away from the mangy fur on Luckhurst's parka. 'I can feel them coming.'

'Hairs! I've got beards; right down to the ground. Hairs on the soles of the feet. Bursting out round the edges. Look, that's not shoe laces down there. That's whiskers.'

'What's the point of doing Hoppo?' said Martin. 'He gets done about once a month. It never stops him.'

'If it hadn't been for Hoppo, Addison wouldn't have won.'

'If it hadn't been for Addison, Hoppo wouldn't have done anything. If it hadn't been for me, no one would have done anything. It won't be Hoppo that gets done over on Monday, I bet.'

'Don't bet,' Forbes pleaded. 'Hey, Traill's only got little legs. If we hung him up he wouldn't touch the ground. Euuuurrugh!' He imitated slow strangulation. 'Surely old Holland won't let Addison win? Not now he knows.'

'He doesn't know how much he knows,' said Martin. 'I bet he's going to do something really nasty.'

'D'you think he'll tell the Head?'

'After he's done it. And he won't do it till four o'clock. He'll keep us in suspense.' The bell rang.

'In that case,' said Forbes, unhooking himself, 'we

don't say anything to the others until he does. We're going to get massacred otherwise. It's geometry next. Think of all those compasses.'

Martin and Forbes sat on their horrible secret all through the first period of geometry, staring with hatred at the back of Addison's smug head, and half-way through the second. Hopkins was very quiet and looked frayed at the edges. Mr Holland was smiling evilly, all the while.

At exactly seventeen minutes to four the bell began to ring and did not stop. Mr Holland's smile became quite ghastly.

'Goodness me,' he said. 'The fire alarm. File out quietly, boys, and assemble on the lower playground. Cheer up, Addison. You're going to miss quite a lot of this nasty maths lesson. Lucky lad!'

Martin looked at Forbes. *Fire alarm?* He imagined a heap of smouldering rags in some secluded waste-paper bin.

'Forbesy, you never...?'

Forbes was grinning too hard to answer. He shook his head.

'Stop talking, Bennett,' said Mr Holland, gaily. 'You might inhale toxic fumes. That boy at the head of the line – where are you going?'

'Lower playground, Sir,' said Luckhurst. 'It says on the notice we have to turn right and go out on the lower playground.'

'The notice? Dammit, Luckhurst, this is an emergency. The stairs are on fire.'

'No they're not, Sir.'

'They are if I say so. Go left, young man, go left. Away from the blazing staircase.'

'But we *are* downstairs,' said Addison, who was skipping about in an agony of frustration. 'Quick, Sir. We got in a row last time for being late out.'

'Addison,' said Mr Holland, 'you are about to be in a row such as you never dreamed of. All rows before and after it will seem as but April showers compared with what you and your mates have got coming to you. I say go left! Left! Left, left, left. I had a good home and I left. Through the cloakroom. Come back, that reckless fool! Addison again? You're leading your comrades to their doom. Good Lord, boy, anyone would think you wanted to get back to your lessons. The quickest way is not always the safest and you'll all be burned to death. Oh dear. What a pity.'

'Why are we running round the wash basins, Sir?' said Hopkins, forlornly. He was limping.

'Sticking close to water,' said Mr Holland. 'Elementary, my dear Hopkins. Round again, please, Luckhurst. You know, Hopkins, I'm surprised you didn't think of this.'

'What, Sir?' said Hopkins. He was beginning to feel picked on.

'The fire alarm, Hopkins. Right up your street, I'd

have thought. Addison wouldn't have stood a chance. Ah! Whose little face do I see among the smoke and flame?'

'What the hell are you doing, Alex?' said Mr Jones, looking round a roller towel.

'We're lost in the smoke and panicking,' said Mr Holland. 'Can you show us the way out?'

'The Old Man's raving in the playground,' said Mr Jones. 'He wanted to clip ten seconds off the existing record.'

'He'll have to wait,' Mr Holland said. 'We are just clipping seventeen minutes off a very different record, aren't we, Addison?'

'I never knew his name was Alex,' Forbes muttered.

'Alexander the Great,' said Martin.

'Do you think he...?'

'*Couldn't* have.'

'Stop talking, Forbes!' Mr Holland shrieked, his voice cracking. 'You'll choke to death. Come along, 1x. Follow Jones! You're not going to die today, after all. Yet.'

On the lower playground the Lower School was drawn up in orderly rows. Up and down the lines the teachers roved with registers, checking to make sure that no one was trapped in the blazing building. In the distance, on the playing field, the Upper School was arranged in the same way, but trying to look dignified about it. The Headmaster was cantering from one group to the other with a stop watch on a string, which he brandished like a knight with a mace and chain when 1x finally filtered out through the double doors and took its place between 1a and 1y.

He directed the full force of his displeasure at Mr Holland, but very discreetly, lest 1x should observe their teacher in trouble and start to enjoy it. Mr Holland, however, beamed throughout. Martin noticed, with a jolt of surprise, that although he was always known as Old Holland he was, in fact, quite young: realized, moreover, that Mr Holland and the Headmaster detested one another and that Mr Holland didn't care: and that he would never tell the Headmaster what had been going on because 1x were his own special headache, and only he could cure it.

1x realized, simultaneously, that they were all fifty pence to the good and wondered what to buy Mr Holland for an end-of-term present, with the exception of Addison, who seemingly writhed with impatience to return to his geometry books.

The fire drill lasted until three minutes to four, and when the school dispersed 1x were detained by Mr Holland who said he wanted a few words with them.

'But not too many words,' he said. 'Because if I kept you after four o'clock, god knows what complications would set in. Four's the deadline and I'm sticking to it. I just wanted you to know that something really frightful is going to happen to you on Monday, and I am going to spend the weekend working it out. If you have any sense you will take whatever I dish out and never refer to this miserable week again. Not a word about chalk, or file paper or Fehling's solution – that's it. Four o'clock. School's over. Hop it.'

They hopped it, with the exception, again, of Addison, who slouched off to the cycle shed to write rude things about Mr Holland, on the wall Martin and Forbes ran after Mr Holland.

'Sir! Sir!'

'Bennett? Forbes?'

'Was it ... did you ... ?'

'There's a fire drill every term, said Mr Holland. 'If you seriously imagine that I arranged it on your rotten behalf...'

'But *seventeen minutes to four*, Sir.'

'Act of God, Bennett. Mr Jones is in charge of fire drill, not me.'

They watched him stroll across the playground to the car park, step into his car and swing it round into the main drive. Near the gate he overtook Mr Jones who was running for his bus. Mr Holland opened the passenger door and beckoned. 'Hop in, Owen.'

Owen.

Alex.

Martin and Forbes exchanged meaning looks. Mr Holland and Mr Jones did not merely compare notes in the Staff Room. They liked each other. They were friends.

In its way, that too was an Act of God.

CHUTZPAH

Eileen had never been into the school before, but she knew the playing field very well, since she had spent most of the Easter holidays lurking in the bushes that grew all round the edge of it. The main gate was in Coldharbour Lane, but Eileen had her own entrance, at the opposite end of the field where the builder's yard was separated from it by nothing more than a bit of stringy fencing, reinforced with barbed wire. Eileen guessed that she was not the only one to use this route, for the stark barbed wire blossomed like the Glaston- bury thorn with multicoloured fragments of wool and serge and denim, where other furtive persons had gone in and out in a hurry.

Auntie Audrey's house was on the corner, next to the builder's yard, so it was the work of ten seconds for Eileen to climb over the garden wall, nip across the yard between the timber stacks, and through the wire. On the first day of term she put on the red and blue bomber jacket, over her brown jeans and the T-shirt with WEST HAM FOR PRESIDENT written across the chest. Then she went over the wall.

It was a pale morning, cloud-coloured, and a shifting haze veiled the school buildings; a haze in which bells rang and whistles blew. That, along with the distant shouts and muffled drumming of unseen feet, put Eileen in mind of a mass breakout from a P.O.W. camp, and the looming hulk of the building began to assume the outlines of Colditz Castle. At any moment she might be flattened by the bruising beam of a searchlight, or brought down in the jaws of a Doberman. A dog did in fact go past, on cue, but it was a bandy, slothful retriever and she knew that it belonged to the caretaker. Being both confirmed lurkers they had met before, in the bushes, and after a brief sniff at her tennis shoes it disappeared into the mist again, nose to the ground.

'Molehound,' said Eileen. Somewhere close by a cement mixer stuttered into life. 'Machine gun,' she said, stooping under a hail of bullets.

Eileen had, in the course of her holiday reconnaissance, located the entrance to the junior cloakrooms, but having to avoid the machine gun fire and watch out for Dobermans, she found it deserted by the time she arrived, and took time off to wash her hands, just to see what the soap was like. The cloakroom smelled reassuringly like the cloakroom at her other school; of feet, and disinfectant, and wet paper towels. Even the soap was exactly the same, left over from last term and as dry as old cheese. It was veined with black deposits. Already there was a moat round the washbasins, and tracks of damp footprints led across the concrete floor and out into the corridor.

'They went thataway,' said Eileen, eyeing the footprints and prepared to sleuth after them, but at that moment a bell rang. Doors slammed, footsteps broke out, punctuated by high-pitched yells and counter-yells from gruff teachers, lower down the scale. Eileen retired to a lavatory, locked herself in and, standing on the seat, peered over the top of the door until she was sure that it was safe to come out; watching a stream of people flood the corridor. While she was peering, a small figure trickled into the cloakroom and concealed itself behind a partition. Eileen waited until silence fell again and then said,

'*I* can see you.'

The figure jumped guiltily and looked round.

'I'm up here,' said Eileen, waving companionably over the top of the door. 'I'd invite you in only there's not really room for more'n one.' She sang: 'But you'd look sweet, upon the seat, of a lavat'ry made for two.'

The guilty loiterer looked more shaken still, then horrified; then burst into tears.

'Nah, don't do that,' Eileen said, remorsefully. 'What's the matter then? Somebody thump you?' She climbed down, unbolted the door and went over to the weeping figure in the corner. It was wearing the shiny striped tie, white blouse and blue pleated skirt of a very new school uniform.

'I should sit down,' said Eileen, clearing a glade among the coats. 'Those are slick shoes,' she said, looking away from her own tennis shoes which had long ago turned the colour of old mushrooms. 'Very nice. Are you new?'

The girl nodded and wiped her nose on the bright white sleeve.

'So'm I. I didn't know you had to wear school uniform.'

'We don't, but they like you to. Weren't you told?' said the girl, looking at WEST HAM FOR PRESIDENT.

'No, I only came here a couple of weeks ago. Never been in here before. What's your name?'

'Lisa Donovan. We moved house and I had to change schools. I could have stayed but my mum said it wasn't worth it, not all that way on the bus. I was at the Montgomery before.'

'Never heard of it. Was it all right?'

'It was better than this dump,' said Lisa, reviving slightly. 'There was only five hundred of us. Sir said there was fourteen hundred here. I bet half the teachers never know who we are.'

'I bet they don't,' Eileen said, thoughtfully. 'You going to hide in here all day?'

'I got lost,' said Lisa. 'They've got two buildings here and I went to the wrong one. I got this far and stopped. I never even found my class.'

'Nor did I,' said Eileen. 'Mind you, I wasn't looking. Let's have a look round while they're all in assembly. We can find our own way.'

They wandered into the corridor. Lisa, regaining confidence, began to get chatty.

'How do you know they're in assembly? Look at that funny painting. Do you think they'll let you wear trousers here? They don't down the Montgomery.'

'I don't care if they don't. I shan't stay if I don't like it,' said Eileen, dusting the seat of her jeans.

'Don't be daft.'

'I shan't. Straight up,' Eileen said. 'Look, all these rooms are for art and craft and that. We only got two at my other school.'

'I'll get into ever such a row if I don't find my class,' Lisa fretted. 'They'll think I'm absent and I won't get any dinner.'

'That mightn't be a bad thing,' Eileen said, darkly. 'How d'you know what it'll be like? Ratburgers, cold greasy chips and gallstones in custard. Hey, there's a sort of oven in that room. D'you think it's a kiln? D'you think they do pottery? I'll stop if I can do pottery. I want to make a thatch cottage for my nan.'

'A cottage?'

'Yes, well; a teapot really,' said Eileen, vaguely. 'Done like a thatch cottage with flowers and that. And the thatch bit comes off and that's the lid. And the chimney's the spout. I saw one in a shop once.'

'Don't you care if you're late?'

'Not really. I can't remember how the handle went, though,' said Eileen. Lisa already had little lines between her eyebrows. A born worrier, Eileen decided.

'What class are you in? I'm in 2a.'

'Dunno,' said Eileen. 'Here, what's that funny box on the wall, looks like a loudspeaker?'

It was a loudspeaker. It spoke.

'Good morning, boys and girls. Welcome back to Shepway School. There will be no assembly this morning...'

'They *aren't* in assembly,' said Lisa. 'Someone'll see us.'

'... as the builders are working in the hall. There will be no pottery classes this term as Mrs Abbott is on maternity leave.'

'Not staying then,' said Eileen.

'The decoration of the Lower School Art Room has taken rather longer than we hoped, so all classes who normally go to that room are to line up quietly in the East Corridor and wait for someone to collect them. The mobile classroom has arrived so there will be no more lessons in the Medical Room. Repeat, *not* in the Medical Room. All those who used to go to the Medical Room will now have their lessons in the new mobile. That's all. Have a good term,' said the loudspeaker heartily, and suspended transmission before anyone had a chance to answer it back.

'Who's that nutter?' said Eileen. 'You're right. This is a dump.'

'That's the Headmaster,' said Lisa. 'I recognize his voice. He's got funny teeth.'

'That's not all he's got funny, if you ask me,' said Eileen. 'Look, *all* these rooms is for craft. The classrooms are over the other side of the playground, in that bit that looks like a milk crate. See all them heads?' Lisa looked through the window. 'And that must be the new mobile.'

'What, that caravan thing with no wheels? I thought a mobile was something you hung up that twiddled round.'

'Some people don't know they're born,' said Eileen. 'Second year already and never been in a mobile!'

This insult went straight over Lisa's head. 'Oh look, they're all coming out. What shall we do? I'll never find my class.' .

'Don't start bawling again,' said Eileen. 'We'll ask someone. They can't all have funny teeth.'

However, before they found someone, someone found them. It was a bearded teacher in a maroon track suit, with a whistle hung round his neck.

'Lost?' he said. 'I'm not surprised. I wish someone would show *me* the way out. Where are you supposed to be?'

'We don't know,' said Eileen. 'That's why we're lost.'

'Are you new?'

'Yes,' said Eileen.

'Then I might suggest that you're not getting off to

a very good start. And you'll wear a skirt in future, please. Girls aren't allowed to wear trousers to school until they're in the fifth year.'

'Can the fifth year boys wear skirts, then?' Eileen asked.

The teacher appeared not to hear this. 'What class are you in?'

'2a,' said Lisa.

'Room 9. First left. And you?'

'2b,' said Eileen, a little too promptly.

'There is no 2b,' said the teacher, sharply. 'You must mean 2v.'

'You got all them classes in one year?' said Eileen.

'Only eight,' he said, 'but they aren't numbered in any way that you'd understand.'

'2v's for the thickies, then,' said Eileen. 'That's me.'

'It's in the bottom corridor, last room,' said the teacher. 'And you'd better hurry up or you'll find they've all gone somewhere else. And *what's* your name, young lady?' he said, to Eileen.

'Julie Smith,' said Eileen.

'I shall remember you, Julie. Now, hurry along.'

They hurried, but Lisa hurried faster.

'Come on, Julie. You heard what he said.'

'My name's not Julie,' said Eileen.

'But you told – '

'That was just tempor'y.'

'What if he finds out?'

'I bet I never see him again,' said Eileen. 'Anyway,

he'll forget. You could see he was a games teacher. That sort only ever remembers the boys.'

'What is your name, then?' Lisa was beginning to look as if she thought there might be safer ways of beginning the day than in Eileen's company.

'Barbara. You can call me Barbie, like the dolls.'

'You don't look like one,' Lisa said.

'Who'd want to look like a Barbie Doll?' said Eileen. 'Except my sister, and she doesn't have any choice. Here's your room, 2a. It's empty.'

Another teacher looked out of a stock room.

'What are you two doing?'

'We're new,' said Eileen. 'We lost our class.'

'All second years have art and craft on Tuesday mornings, but you'll be split up into groups. You'd better run along and see who can fit you in.'

'Split up – fitted in – anyone'd think we was luggage,' Eileen muttered.

'Please Miss,' Lisa cut in hurriedly, 'my teacher doesn't know I'm here. I won't be on the dinner register.'

'Then go down to the office and sort it out.'

'Where's the office?' said Eileen. 'We're new – '

'Down the steps, through the entrance hall, first right and hurry!'

'Don't hurry,' Eileen cautioned, as soon as they were out of earshot. 'You'll only get in a flap again. Here we are. I'll wait.'

'What about you?'

'I'll go home for lunch,' said Eileen. 'Probably.'

Lisa sorted out her problems with the school secretary and emerged, looking much happier.

'She's ever so nice, that secretary lady,' Lisa said. 'She told me not to get upset *and* she found the 2a register and marked me present. You ought to get her to find yours.'

'I don't know what class I'm in, yet, do I?'

'That teacher said 2v.'

'He said he *thought* 2v. I want to have a look at them, first,' said Eileen. 'See all them cups in that glass case? Fancy leaving them out here. Back at my other school, somebody'd nick 'em.'

'I should think you were glad to leave that school,' Lisa said, frankly. 'Come on, Barbie. We'd better get over to that art place and find our class.'

'Cool it,' said Eileen, but she peeled herself away from the wall and followed Lisa, back the way they had come earlier, to the corridor where they had taken their first look round. Before they reached it they could hear sounds of strife and complaint and when they turned the corner they ran into a fractious crowd of about thirty people, shoving up against a locked door.

'Here,' said one girl. 'The Art Room's full of men.'

'What d'you mean, full?' said another. 'I can only see two and that little Indian's Sudesh's brother. He only left school last year. You can't count him. I don't call that full.'

'This must be that room we got to line up quietly outside of,' said Eileen. Lisa shrank back against the wall, unwilling to be sucked into the vortex, as one huge fellow, head and shoulders higher than the rest, flung himself at the door and began hammering on it.

'Where's Miss? We want Miss! We want Miss! We want – '

'Shuddup, Hawkins,' said the first girl. 'Mrs Abbott's having a baby.'

'What, in there?' said Eileen.

'Sir said she was on maternity leave,' said Hawkins, pausing in mid-howl.

'That *means* having a baby, Dumbo,' said the girl who had identified Sudesh's short brother.

'Who are you, anyway?' said her sidekick, squaring up to Eileen. 'Who asked you to butt in? Who do you think you are?'

'Princess Anne,' said Eileen. 'And the band played *Believe It If You Like*. Who are you?'

'I'm Helen Shovelar, that's who. And *she's* Sharon Atwell.' Evidently this meant something, for the rest of the group drew back, respectfully. 'So what are you going to do about it?'

'Perhaps this isn't our group,' Lisa said, hopefully. 'It doesn't look like our group.'

'West Ham's rubbish,' said Hawkins, catching sight of Eileen's slogan.

'It looks like *my* group,' said Eileen. 'Hey, belt up, you lot. Here comes the Old Bill.'

'You what?' said Sharon. 'That's Mr Ager. Who *are* you, anyway?'

'All teachers are Old Bill round our way,' said Eileen, and down the corridor came Old Bill Ager, swinging a T-square.

'Any more of that row,' he said, with a swipe that made the T-square sing like a saw, 'and you'll all go and wait outside. Stop trying to climb up the door, Hawkins. You'll never make it. Now, what seems to be the trouble?'

'There's all these men in the Art Room,' said Sharon, 'and we're locked out.'

'The Art Room's being decorated, as you can very well see,' said Mr Ager, 'and not ten minutes ago the Headmaster told you so. He also told you to wait *quietly* until you were collected.'

'But we haven't been collected, Sir.'

'Thank you, Helen. I can see that and I should think that the rest of the school had guessed. Something's gone horribly wrong,' he said, 'as usual. Are you all one class?'

'Not likely,' said Sharon. 'We're 2h. Them boys is 2v.'

'I'm 2a,' said Lisa, but no one heard.

'Then you'd better queue up outside my room in SILENCE until I find somewhere to put you. NOW!'

The mob unravelled itself until it was strung out in a lumpy line along the corridor. Eileen and Lisa found themselves at the head of it, by the open door of Mr Ager's room. Eileen looked in.

'You lot aren't coming in here,' said one of the boys inside, sticking his head round the door. A second head joined the first.

'What's all them girls doing out there?'

Eileen made an oriental gesture, suggestive of broken necks.

'Why don't you come and find out?'

The owner of the head, who was rather smaller than Eileen, withdrew hastily, taking his head with him. 'We ain't having no girls in woodwork.'

'Who's keeping me out? You?'

'I don't hit *girls*.'

'If I was your size I wouldn't hit anyone,' Eileen advised him. Lisa tugged at her arm.

'Don't let's stay here. I want to find my class.'

'I don't.' Eileen looked round at the crew behind her. 'This lot's all right, and you heard what that teacher said – we're all muddled up, anyway. Groups, she said, but she meant muddled up. It doesn't matter where we go. They might let us do woodwork.'

'With all those boys in there? I don't want to do woodwork,' said Lisa. 'Ssssh. He's coming back; with a lady.'

'Is that what you call a straight line?' said Mr Ager, knocking it into shape with the T-square. '*Silent?* Right, now listen, there's been a hitch. Several hitches, so we'll just have to do the best we can.' He counted heads. 'How come so many boys in one group – just my luck.'

'Sixty-eight was a bad year,' Eileen murmured.

'That's enough of that. What's your name?'

'Susan Tucker,' said Eileen. 'I'm new.'

'Not too new to do as you're told. Right, two-four-six-eight-nine... You lads get across to Mr Milne, for technical drawing. He's going to fit you in with his C.S.E. class. The rest of the boys stay with me for woodwork. We'll manage somehow, but no one is to touch the lathe. Girls, go with Miss Turner, here. Right? Well GO ON!' he bellowed, and lowering the T-square he putted his victims into the room and slammed the door.

2

'Shall we get on up to your room, Miss?' said Sharon, as soon as the door was closed.

'We're not using my room,' said Miss Turner. 'There's a maths class in it this period. We'll have to make do with Room F for now. You all know where that is, don't you?'

There came a sustained moan of agreement from the rest of the group. Clearly, everybody knew where Room F was, and what it was.

'We don't, please, Miss,' said Eileen. 'We're new.'

'So I gathered,' said Miss Turner, in a voice that

was not calculated to make newcomers feel welcome. 'All right, girls; Room F's in the old building, but we'll have to go the long way round to avoid the builders. Follow me.'

'What's the old building like, if this is the new one?' Eileen wondered loudly as they followed Miss Turner out of the door and across a rubble-strewn wasteland where defunct central heating boilers rusted in the mud like abandoned tanks. 'My grandad's garden used to look like this – but he let it go down hill.'

They went in at another door and up a staircase where a notice said DO NOT GO UP THIS STAIR-CASE. Someone had scribbled underneath *Use the drainpipe*. At the top, on the landing, was a row of desks.

'Is this your room, Miss?' Eileen asked.

'This is where the fifth form works,' said Miss Turner. 'Now, I don't want any noise going down this corridor; lessons have started. Go straight to the end, down the stairs, and wait for me at the bottom.'

'Roll up for the Magical Mystery Tour,' said Eileen.

'I beg your pardon?' said Miss Turner who did not, as it happened, look as though she would do anything of the kind.

'Well, we come up, and we go down,' said Eileen, 'and we go round the houses...'

'We can't use the lower corridor because the builders have the floor up. Now, if you have any more complaints, I suggest you go back where you came from.'

'See if I don't,' Eileen said, under her breath, and followed Miss Turner, but slowly, so that by the time they had reached the middle of the corridor she had worked her way to the back of the line.

'You'll get into ever such trouble if you keep cheeking the teachers,' said Lisa.

'Who's cheeking them? It's always the same; they can say what they like to us, but all we can say is Yes Miss.'

'*You* don't.'

'Yes I do. If I'm spoke nicely to,' said Eileen.

'That Sharon's giving you funny looks.'

'Let her.' Eileen glared at Sharon. 'I've seen people's eyes drop out, doing that.'

'I should think anyone's eyes would drop out, looking at you,' said the loyal Helen.

'Sticks and stones may break my bones,' said Eileen, 'but words will just make me turn nasty, and you ain't seen nothing yet.'

'Now,' said Miss Turner, at the foot of the stairs, 'it's the room at the end of the corridor. The door's open. Go straight in.'

'Hey!' said Eileen. 'It's a cloakroom.'

It was, too. All round the walls were hooks and shoe racks and at one end, a row of washbasins. A black hot-water pipe came up out of the floor and ran the length of the room before disappearing into the wall, at exactly the right height to trip people up. In the middle of the concrete floor a dozen desks huddled together as if for warmth, like cows in a windswept pasture.

'All mod cons,' said Miss Turner, defensively. 'No one else has six washbasins.'

'They got windows though,' said Sharon. All the windows here were in the ceiling; yellowing skylights with grimy cracks across them, just like the cloakroom soap. Everyone sat down. Eileen stood up.

'Excuse me, Miss. Do you mind if I say something?'

''Scuse *me*, Miss,' Sharon mimicked silently. 'What's all this *'scuse me?* Don't you take no notice, Miss. She'll say it anyway, whether you mind or not. She's nothing to do with us. *I've* never seen her before.'

'She's new,' said a dark girl, with long black plaits. 'She says.'

'Thank you Davinda. I think we all know that now,' said Miss Turner. 'All right, what's-your-name; Susan. What did you want to say? Susan!'

Eileen jumped. She had forgotten that she was currently Susan Tucker. So had Lisa, who was poking her nervously and mumbling, 'Go on, Barbie.'

'Oh, well, Miss, I was just going to say I didn't think it was fair.'

'Fair?' said Miss Turner. 'Of course it's not fair. What have I done to deserve being stuck in this hole?'

'I didn't mean that,' Eileen said. 'I mean, it wasn't fair us having to come over here.'

'Right again. This is my double free period – my only free period,' said Miss Turner, heavily. 'And what happens? I lose it on the first day of term. You're so right it's not fair.'

'Yes, Miss,' said Eileen, patiently, 'but what I meant was, it isn't fair the way we was sorted out. I mean, boys go here and boys go there, and girls,' she said witheringly, '*girls* go over here. All together. I mean, he should have asked us where we wanted to go.'

'Why should anyone ask you?' said Sharon. 'You're not even in our class. She's 2v, Miss. Push off.'

'I'm in this *group*,' said Eileen. 'And so's my mate, Lisa.'

'That's enough, you two,' said Miss Turner. 'You were sent here because it's an emergency, and if you'd been allowed to choose, no one would have chosen to come over here, now would they? Messrs Ager and Milne would have been swamped with eager little woodworkers and technical draughtsmen.'

'Technical draughtswomen,' said Eileen. '*No they wouldn't*. That's the point. They wouldn't have us in their rooms even if we asked to go. Never mind if we wanted to do woodwork, they wouldn't let us. That's what's not fair. Mr Ager said, sort of, that there was too many boys, but he didn't send *them* over here, did he? He didn't ask *us*, did he? He didn't – '

'He didn't ask me, either,' said Miss Turner.

'It's all right, Miss. Don't take no notice of her,' said Davinda, consolingly. 'She's not in our class.'

'Nor am I,' said Lisa. 'I'm in 2a.'

'2a's doing needlework,' said Helen.

'Well go and do needlework, then,' said Miss Turner. 'At this rate there'll be no time to do anything. And you can go too, Susan.'

'I want to do woodwork,' said Eileen. 'It's just the same at my other school. Boys do woodwork and girls do sewing. Boys do metalwork, girls do cookery. I mean, Miss, even if this wasn't an emergency, they still wouldn't let me, would they?'

'They might if enough girls wanted to do it,' said Miss Turner. 'But I don't think any of them do.'

'*I* don't,' said Helen. 'And I don't want to do technical drawing. All them nuts and bolts.'

'But suppose you want to do an apprenticeship when you leave school,' said Eileen. 'Suppose you want to be a tool maker – something like that – skilled, like.'

Helen looked thrown, but not for long.

'I'm going to be a children's nurse. Do you know what they make in woodwork, clever-clogs? Matchbox holders and garden lines. All my brothers is at this school. We got four matchbox holders and three garden lines at home. Brian's in the first year and he's still making his garden line. We haven't even got a garden.'

'It's better than making woolly bird-bath cosies,' said Eileen. 'Here, Miss, if I got up a petition, d'you reckon they'd let us do it?'

'They? Who would you take a petition to?' asked Miss Turner. 'Assuming that anyone signed it.'

'The Headmaster,' said Eileen. 'I bet lots of girls would like to do it, but they never thought they could. You'd like to do woodwork, wouldn't you, Lisa?'

'I want to get to my needlework,' said Lisa.

'Both of you can go to needlework,' said Miss Turner. 'This minute!' She turned away and began taking stationery out of a drawer. Sharon sprang up officiously and cleaned the rickety blackboard with extravagant vigour. All the girls sat and looked at Miss Turner with virtuous smirks, studiously ignoring the two outcasts.

'It's illegal,' said Eileen, lingering, as Lisa headed for the door.

'What's illegal?'

'Not letting us. Straight up it is.'

'Send in the Sweeney,' said Helen. 'Ten years for Sir.'

'*Can* I get up a petition, Miss?'

'If anyone gets up a petition it'll be me,' said Sharon, who had been unexpectedly silent during the previous exchange of opinion.

'You don't want to do woodwork,' said Helen.

'Who says? Anyway, I'm head of this form. Petitions is my job.'

'You going to take it to Sir?' Davinda jeered. 'After what happened when you come to school with green hair?'

'You shut your face!' Sharon lunged across the desk, apparently bent on settling an old score. 'Just 'cause Mrs Buckley lets you polish her rubber plant you think – '

'You want a knuckle sandwich?' Davinda bellowed, twitching her plaits out of reach.

'Sharon, sit down at once. Sharon! Davinda, really,' Miss Turner protested. 'Didn't I hear you'd been chosen for the choral speaking competition?'

Davinda beamed. 'Who told you that, Miss?'

'Mrs Buckley, and she was so pleased. What would she say if she heard you speaking like that?'

'She'd be pleased I was talking English so good,' Davinda said, cheerfully.

Eileen and Lisa slipped out before anyone remembered who had started the row. As they were climbing the stairs to go back to the new building, a bell rang.

'That's a whole lesson gone and we haven't done anything,' Lisa wailed. 'They'll be furious when we get there.'

'They don't even know we're here yet,' said Eileen. 'They don't even know we exist. If I was you, I'd miss the rest of the lesson and just turn up next week. Say you was late or something – say you had to go to the doctor, I always do. I'm not going to needlework anyway. It's not my class.'

'That 2v was your class.'

'I don't think it was,' said Eileen. 'I mean, they never said definitely I was in 2v, did they? It might have been 2c or 2d or 2p or 2t. Funny how many letters sound like 'ee', isn't it? I don't think I'll go anywhere till after break. See you around.'

'I think you're barmy,' Lisa said, enviously, and broke into a run.

Eileen continued down the corridor at a more leisurely pace. At the sound of the bell, doors had opened all the way along it, and people were dodging in and out with the anxious and mistrustful expressions of those who play musical chairs, as if convinced that there would be one classroom fewer than there were classes. On the landing the desks were now occupied by hefty fifth formers, who glowered at Eileen as she fetched up beside them.

'No infants allowed up here,' said an elderly-looking boy with a precocious stubble on his chin and some kind of badge in his lapel. 'Push off, titch.'

'Are you the Gaffer?' Eileen propped herself against a vacant desk. 'Do you really have to work out here?'

'We're supposed to,' said another boy with a Manchester United scarf round his neck. He was setting up a bowling alley with ten empty milk bottles and a balding tennis ball. 'What's it got to do with you, anyway? West Ham's rubbish. Push off.'

'Go back down the lower side,' said one of the girls

who was wearing that sign of female seniority – trousers.

'I'm fourth year,' said Eileen. 'I'm just small for my age. I had this bone disease when I was little.'

'You're still little,' said the bowling expert. 'Go away.'

Eileen prepared to settle in and sat down on the desk, legs swinging. 'I'm new. I can't find my class.'

'You might try looking for it,' said the girl in the trousers. 'Damn – I left all my maths books in the cloakroom. Anybody here got theirs?'

Nobody had.

'I suppose you can't leave your books out here in case they get nicked,' said Eileen. 'That wouldn't happen if you had a proper classroom, would it? Why d'you put up with it?'

'Because there's nowhere else to go, that's why,' said the bowler. 'On the other hand, there's lots of places you could go. Over the banisters, for a start. Want a leg up?'

'You ought to write to the papers,' said Eileen, ' and expose conditions.'

'What's the point? Everyone round here knows what it's like already.'

'I didn't mean the local paper,' said Eileen. 'I meant one of the big ones, you know, the *Mirror* or something. You might get a reporter down. You'd get your name in the paper, and photographs. You might get on telly.'

'He's had his name in the paper,' said the Gaffer. 'He breeds ferrets. They win prizes.'

'I got a rat at home,' said Eileen. 'It's called Rover. But no, I meant it. I mean, at my other school we was having lessons in the cycle shed, some of the time, and a lot of the parents got together and wrote to the papers and in the end we had the Inspectors in. It would look much worse if *you* wrote to the papers.'

'Oh yeah? And what do you think Tarzan would say to that?'

'Who's Tarzan?' said Eileen. 'The Education Officer? It's no good writing to him.'

'You know a lot about it, don't you? We got a proper little barrack-room lawyer here,' said Bowler, to the rest of the group. 'Tarzan's the Headmaster on account of he's five foot six with contact lenses. One fell out in his tea once,' he said, with a smile of happy reminiscence. 'We thought it was his eye.'

A hollow moan interrupted him. It was the loudspeaker.

'I should like to point out,' it said, 'that boys and girls are forbidden to annoy the builders at break time...'

'Any other time but never break,' said Bowler.

'... it is extremely dangerous to interfere with their equipment...'

'Norman the Foreman's been complaining again,' said the girl in trousers.

'... apologize to teachers for disturbing their lessons. Thank you.'

'That's Tarzan,' said the Gaffer. 'Hear that thumping in the background? He's beating his chest.'

'I heard him this morning,' said Eileen, 'chatting about rooms. Here – ' she suddenly remembered which rooms he had been chatting about. 'I know a place where you can go.'

'And I know a place where *you* can go,' said Bowler. The tennis ball skidded, missed all the bottles and went off by itself downstairs, b-dump, b-dump, b-dump. 'Fffffff...' said Bowler.

'No, straight up,' said Eileen. 'Didn't you hear what he said, this morning, about the Medical Room?'

'Medical Room's in Lower School,' said Bowler. 'What were you doing in Lower School if you're supposed to be fourth year?'

'I was lost,' said Eileen. 'Still am, come to that. No, listen; he said there wouldn't be any more lessons in the Medical Room because the new mobile's arrived.'

'Big deal,' said Bowler. 'We ought to have got that mobile and they go and give it to little juniors.'

'Ah, yes,' said Eileen. 'But that means the Medical Room's empty doesn't it? Why don't you move in there?'

'Hark at her,' said the Gaffer. 'Why don't we move 'n there? I'll tell you why we don't move in there.

Because we aren't allowed to move in there, that's why.'

'Aren't allowed?' said Eileen. 'That's not the way to get things done. You want to take it over, mate. Have a sit-in.'

'You have a sit-in,' said the girl in the trousers. 'Go and sit in the dustbin.'

'It's no good waiting for the Bosses to give you what you want,' said Eileen. 'You could wait forever. These days you got to take what you're entitled to. You go and see Tarzan about that Medical Room, and if he says no, you occupy it.' She stood up and prepared to move off. 'You won't get nothing done if you just sit here and belly-ache about it.'

'Bleedin' Joan of Arc,' said Bowler, as Eileen went downstairs, but he sounded less disdainful already. Eileen retrieved his tennis ball from under a radiator and chucked it back up the stair well. There came a melodious chiming of milk bottles followed by the return of the tennis ball on its way down again, b-dump, b-dump. She had scored a direct hit.

3

Eileen put in a little lurking at break, between the dustbins and the plunging concrete staircase that went down to the boiler room. From here she could observe all the coming and going, and much that went on in between. Lisa had taken up with a washed-out, monochrome creature, exactly like herself which was just, Eileen thought, what you might expect to find in a needlework class. Helen and Sharon had convened a strong-arm mob and were going about inviting people to sign Sharon's petition. Davinda, using her long plaits as a knout, was recruiting a posse to duff up Helen and Sharon, while great big Hawkins was running away from three little girls who seemed to fancy him or perhaps simply enjoyed frightening him.

The fifth form, whose landing window was just above Eileen's dug-out and betrayed by an open window, were drafting a strongly worded communiqué to the Headmaster, on the subject of the vacant Medical Room. Eileen's person was not mentioned, but she gathered that her influence was beginning to make itself felt.

Towards the end of break she emerged to make a few inquiries, beginning with Davinda.

'What's 2h got after break?' Eileen said.

'Why should you care?' said Davinda. 'You ain't in 2h.'

'I don't know what I'll be in yet,' said Eileen. 'I haven't made me mind up.'

'Go and ask at the office,' said Davinda. 'We got maths next.'

'I'm not in 2h, then,' said Eileen, and went after Hawkins. 'Here Hawkins, I'll save you. What have 2v got after break?'

'Geography,' said Hawkins. 'Look, get out of it, will you?' he said, to the little girls who had fastened on him like crocodile clips. 'They want to kiss me!' he said to Eileen, outraged.

'Well never mind. I don't,' said Eileen, and wandered off to find Lisa, basely abandoning him to his fate.

'West Ham's rubbish!' Hawkins yelled, vengefully.

'Ho! What do you support, *Millwall?*'

'How did you know?' Hawkins was taken aback.

'You can spot Millwall supporters a mile off,' said Eileen. 'It's the pointed heads that give you away . . .'

Lisa and pale friend had already reached the stage of shlumping round the playground with their arms across each other's shoulders.

'This is Sarah,' said Lisa. 'Sarah, this is Barbie. She doesn't know what class she's in.'

The friend sucked in a great wad of lower lip under her front teeth and tittered, ih-ih-ih-ih, like a ping-pong ball; let go of her lip and said, breathily, 'You're not supposed to wear trousers.'

'Exciting friends you've got,' said Eileen. 'A thrill-a-minute. How do you stand the pace? What's your class doing after break?'

'It's meant to be singing with 2r,' said Sarah, 'but the timetable's been changed. We've got English now and singing tomorrow, first period after lunch.'

'I don't think I'll be here tomorrow,' said Eileen 'Who's got singing instead of you?'

Sarah thought about this, which took a long time.

While she was thinking a whistle blew and she began to wander away, still hooked round Lisa's neck.

'Oy!' said Eileen. 'When're you going to tell me? Wednesday week?'

'Third year,' said Sarah. 'Must be third year because they should have singing tomorrow but we had to change places with them because their English teacher's got to take games while Miss McKenna's covering for Mrs Abbott – '

'Who's having a baby,' Eileen prompted.

' – only it might be fourth year because Mr Singh's taking science this term till Mr Adams gets back.'

'Is he having a baby too?' asked Eileen. 'Where's the singing lesson?'

Sarah took another deep breath. 'Well, it should be in the hall but the builders are in the hall taking all the pipes out and I saw Mr Harper and Fred Tovey pushing the piano down the canteen. So it's probably in the canteen. Anyway, what's it got to do with you? You aren't in the third year.'

'I might be,' said Eileen. 'I'll see what they're like, first, though. Which way's the canteen?'

'Through there.' Sarah pointed. 'But you mustn't go that way because of the builders.'

'Norman the Foreman?'

Up came a teacher in a track suit, with a whistle round his neck. Eileen looked elaborately in the other direction, but it was a different track suit, a different whistle, a different teacher: unless he had shaved off his beard.

'What are you girls doing out here?' he demanded. 'Didn't you hear the whistle? Go to your classes at once.'

Lisa and Sarah scuttled off, still gibbering, and Eileen heard Lisa's voice fading away. '... honestly, she's *bonkers*.'

'I'm new,' said Eileen. 'I don't know where to go.'

'Do you know where you ought to be?' said the teacher. He was young and very good looking. Eileen made sheep's eyes at him, since she could see it was what he was used to.

'In the canteen, Sir, for singing.'

'Singing in the canteen?' he said. 'Are you sure?'

Eileen had an excellent memory, when she cared to use it. 'Well, Sir, it should be the hall but the builders are in there taking the pipes out and I saw Mr Harper and Fred Tovey pushing the piano down the canteen so I thought we ought to be in there because we had to change places with 2a because our English teacher's got to take games while Miss McKenna's covering for Mrs Abbott so we're having singing today and they're having it tomorrow.'

'I thought you said you were new,' said the teacher. 'You seem to know a lot about it.'

'I come at the end of last term, Sir,' said Eileen, hurriedly. 'I'm not new today, Sir.'

'Then you should know better than to turn up at

school wearing trousers,' he said. 'Only the fifth year girls can do that.'

'Yes Sir. Sorry Sir.' Eileen looked abjectly at the ground, which gave her a chance to see if she might reach the doorway before he did, should she decide to make a dash for it. 'I have got a skirt, Sir, but my auntie had an accident, last night.'

'An accident?' He looked properly concerned.

'Yes, Sir. I live with my auntie, Sir, and she was ironing my skirt and the iron was too hot and it went ever so small and all sticky, Sir.'

'The iron?'

'No, my skirt,' said Eileen. 'Can I go to singing now, please?' she added. 'I don't want to miss it.'

'What class are you in?'

'3a, I think, Sir,' Eileen said, cautiously.

'3a have games now,' he said. 'In fact, I'm waiting for them.'

'Oh, well, it was 3a last term, Sir, only the Headmaster said I was in the wrong class and I might have to be moved because there was too many of us and I forget which one he said.'

'Which class were you in before break?'

'I wasn't here before break,' said Eileen. 'I had to go to the doctor about my verrucas. I *know* I've got singing now, Sir. My mate told me. In the canteen.'

'Hurry up, then,' said the teacher. 'And you'd better make sure you've got the right class. If you haven't, go and see the secretary. She'll sort you out.

No, not that way,' he shouted, as Eileen sprinted off towards the distant canteen. 'Didn't you hear what the Headmaster told you about not going anywhere near the builders?'

'I thought that was only at break,' said Eileen. 'Which way should I go?'

'Round past the science lab,' he answered. She thought for a moment that he was going to come after her, but at that moment 3a came whooping out of the door, across the playground, and diverted his attention by landing a javelin on the roof.

She had no idea where the science lab was, but now that no one was watching it seemed safe to cut across the building site. It was the no-man's-land they had traversed earlier with Miss Turner. On her right was the entrance to the Upper School in the old building, but from the left she could hear the insistent thumping of a piano, and ragged voices crooning, 'A safe stronghohold our Gohod is still, a trusty shield ahand weahehepon...'

Eileen suddenly realized that she was not in the singing class after all and turned right, into the Upper School, where she was immediately pounced upon by yet another teacher.

'And what do you think you're doing, wandering about in the middle of lessons?'

'Wandering about in the middle of lessons,' Eileen

murmured, before turning round. 'I'm new, please Miss,' she said aloud. 'I'm looking for the – the – library,' she went on, noticing the word LIBRARY painted on the nearest door.

'What do you want the library for?'

'Mrs Buckley sent me,' said Eileen.

'Really?' said the teacher. 'I'm Mrs Buckley.'

'Oh,' said Eileen.

'I don't remember sending you anywhere,' said Mrs Buckley, who had one single fascinating whisker growing out of her chin. Eileen thought rapidly and fixed her eyes on the whisker. 'I don't remember seeing you before at all. What's your name?'

'Deborah Clark,' said Eileen.

'And what class are you in, Deborah?'

'2v,' said Eileen and went up on her toes, ready to run.

'Oh, you mean Mrs Buckmaster,' said Mrs Buckley. 'In the geography room.'

'That's right, Miss.' Eileen could hardly believe her luck. All her pent-up breath escaped in a gust of relief, and Mrs Buckley's whisker trembled, slightly. 'I must have got mixed up, Miss, being new and that. I got to get this special atlas, Miss. Where is the library, Miss?'

'Right in front of you,' said Mrs Buckley. 'The geography section's down at the back.' She stood and watched until Eileen had safely covered the three yards between herself and the door of the library. Eileen paused at the door.

'Can I polish your rubber plant, Miss? I can take turns with Davinda.'

'No you can not – and how do you come to know Davinda so well if you're new?'

'She lives up our street,' said Eileen. 'You ought to give me a try, Miss. You should see what I done to my auntie's Swiss Cheese plant. It's got the biggest holes – '

'That's enough, Deborah. Go and find your atlas,' said Mrs Buckley, and moved up close to the door where she stood watching while Eileen successfully negotiated the remainder of the journey to the geography section, before turning away.

Eileen waited until she could no longer hear footsteps and then went to look round. The library was empty except for two seniors playing poker behind the encyclopaedias, and Eileen took her time about looking for the special atlas, until she remembered that it probably didn't exist, and that even if it did, neither she nor Mrs Buckmaster wanted it. She found a tin of paper clips instead, and made two chains to adorn herself with. By this time the sky had darkened and a thin rain was spitting against the windows. One of the seniors got up to switch on the lights and the other sneaked a look at his cards. It was warm and peaceful in the library, and even when the bell rang for change-of-lesson, no one came in to disturb them. In the biology section Eileen discovered a tatty paperback in a brown cover, that turned out to be called *The Swiftly Beating Heart*, by one Erin O'Mara. It had nothing to do with biology, however, and Eileen settled down for a quiet read until lunch time.

The canteen, vacated by the singers, was now full of hungry people and the smell of food A row of water jugs stood on the piano. Eileen, head still ringing with Miss O'Mara's hot prose, joined the queue behind Lisa and Sarah, who were wittering with Davinda.

'Where's your loony friend?' Davinda asked.

'Don't look round now,' said Eileen, over her shoulder.

Davinda was unabashed.

'You decided what class you're in yet?'

'I was in the library, last period,' said Eileen. 'It's nice, that library. They leave you alone.'

'*We* was in the library last period,' said Davinda, swiftly. 'I never saw you.'

'I was in the Upper School library; I'm third year, now,' Eileen said.

'I suppose you'll be fourth year this afternoon, ih-ih-ih-ih,' said Sarah.

'And Headmaster tomorrow,' said Davinda. 'What happens when they find out what you been up to?'

'It'll be too late,' said Eileen with a cryptic smile

'Anyone got games this afternoon? I like games.' Their part of the queue had drawn level with the serving hatch. 'See, I told you. Ratburgers.'

'2a's got games tomorrow,' said Sarah.

'I might drop in.'

'Here,' said Davinda, 'what's that you got on your ears?'

'Paper clips,' said Eileen. 'Never heard of a clip round the ear?'

They could sit anywhere they liked, it seemed, but there were very few empty seats left, and after they had sat down Eileen was alarmed to notice that the next table was occupied by teachers. She bent low over her ratburger.

'I thought you said you were going home to dinner,' said Lisa.

'I changed my mind, didn't I?'

'Whose dinner register are you on?' Davinda asked, sharply. 'If you haven't got a class you can't be on a dinner register.'

'I must be on somebody's register,' said Eileen, 'so that's all right, isn't it?'

'But you'll be marked absent, won't you?' said Sarah, after a long pause for thought.

'She *won't* be on a register if they don't know she's here,' said Davinda. 'Will she? She ought to tell someone she's here before she has any dinner.'

'Oh well, it doesn't matter,' said Eileen. 'I have free dinners anyway.'

'I bet you don't,' said Davinda.

'This one's free, isn't it?' Familiar voices from the next table caught her attention. 'Ssssh, a minute.'

'And what was the fight about?' Miss Turner was saying.

'A petition, if you please,' said Mrs Buckley. 'Sharon Atwell's got up this petition about girls doing woodwork and she's taking it round the school. The trouble is, she's beating up anyone who won't sign it – which is most of the boys, of course.'

'I never knew Sharon was interested in woodwork,' said Mr Ager. 'I never knew Sharon was interested in anything.'

'She isn't,' said Miss Turner. 'Well, not in anything that *we* teach, at any rate. It was that new girl who set her off – Susan Tucker.'

'Oh, her,' said Mr Ager. 'The one with jeans and her tongue hung in the middle. Didn't I send her to you?'

'Yes,' said Miss Turner, 'and I sent her to needlework.'

'Well, she never arrived,' said Mrs Buckley. 'Wait a moment, did you say a new girl – in jeans?'

'That's right; the West Ham supporter. She couldn't find her class.'

'West Ham?' said Mrs Buckley, curiously. 'What colour hair; not red, was it?'

'Yes, and very short. Is she one of yours?' said Mr Ager.

'No she isn't, praise be,' said Mrs Buckley. 'But I met her in the Upper School after break. She said she was in 2v and her name was Deborah Clark.'

'Oh, did she?' said another voice. It was the bearded games teacher. 'Well, her name was Julie Smith at a quarter past nine, this morning.'

'Red hair and jeans?' said someone else. 'West Ham? She's in the third year. I saw her after break, looking for the canteen.'

'Hey, Barbie, they're talking about you,' said Lisa. 'You'll cop it now.'

Eileen laid her knife and fork together, neatly, and stood up.

'I don't think I'll wait for afters,' she said. 'See you around, maybe,' and slid discreetly into the crowd that was waiting to leave the canteen.

'Good heavens,' said Mrs Buckley, in the distance. 'There she goes.'

The bearded teacher leaped to his feet. 'Come back, that girl!'

Eileen put out her elbows and shamelessly barged her way to the door, noticing in passing that Sharon Atwell had a black eye coming.

'Who d'you think you're shoving?' said Helen. 'Oh, it's you, is it? West Ham's rubbish.'

'Women and children first,' said Eileen, 'and I'm both.' She burst through the double doors and began to run across the building site, narrowly missing an early death in a cement mixer, and ricochetting off the prow of a whale-shaped gentleman in a donkey jacket who had to be Norman the Foreman. But the bearded teacher was not a games master for nothing. He caught up with Eileen before she was two thirds of the way across and, dodging from foot to foot like a boxer, he manoeuvred her indoors.

'Now,' he said.

'Sir?' said Eileen.

'I think you've got some explaining to do, don't you, whatever-your-name-is?'

'Yes, Sir,' said Eileen. Who would have thought he could move so fast?

'Well, what *is* your name, for a start?'

'Eileen Skeates,' said Eileen, off guard and running short of ideas.

'*Skates?*'

'Skeates.'

'That's a new one. Is it true?'

'Oh yes,' said Eileen. 'Eileen Marie Skeates. That's my real name.'

'Then why do you go round calling yourself Julie Smith and Deborah Clark and – what was the other one?'

'Susan Tucker.'

'Why did you?'

'I dunno, Sir.'

'And which class are you in?'

'Dunno, Sir.'

'Why didn't you find out? It wouldn't have taken long.'

'Dunno, Sir. I was late, see, and I didn't know where to go and everything was in such a muddle...'

'Ah, yes,' he said. 'Members of staff away, builders in some rooms, decorators in others. We don't usually get into this kind of a muddle and when we do, we don't expect some tiresome little girls to go adding to the chaos.'

'No, Sir,' said Eileen, all humble.

'And no one told you which class you were in before you came?'

'Well, I haven't lived round here long and my auntie, what I live with, Sir, didn't know what to do, so she said I should just turn up and ask,' said Eileen, in her orphaned voice.

'Did she now?' said Sir. 'I think the best thing you can do is to go and see the Headmaster and we'll let him sort it out.'

'Oh, yes, Sir,' said Eileen, brightening. 'Where is his room, Sir?'

'First left at the top of the stairs – no. On second thoughts,' he said, 'I'll come with you. I shouldn't like you to get lost again. Come along. Keep moving.'

It had struck Eileen, while he was talking, that a riot seemed to be developing in the near distance, and as they went through the entrance hall *en route* for the staircase, they ran into the outskirts of an argument that was being waged round a half-open door labelled MEDICAL ROOM. Someone was striving to force his way in against what appeared to be superior numbers who were trying to hold the door shut, while an angry crowd surged about in the corridor.

'What the devil's going on here?' Sir demanded, and hurled himself into the mêlée just as Bowler burst out of it. Eileen oozed quietly away.

Avoiding the building site and making a law-abiding detour round the science lab, she ran into Lisa and Sarah, with Davinda in tow.

'What'd he say, then?' said Davinda. 'What's he going to do to you?'

'I got to see the Headmaster,' said Eileen.

'When?'

'Now, I suppose.'

'So where are you going? This isn't the way to his room. This is the way out.'

'Yes,' said Eileen. 'I'm, going home.'

Sarah and Lisa drew deep, disapproving breaths, simultaneously. 'Ummmm!'

'You'll get into ever such trouble if you go wagging it now,' Sarah said. 'You'll get suspended or something.'

'No,' said Eileen. 'I got to go home. I got to get back to school on Thursday.'

'What you mean?' said Davinda. 'What you mean, back to school? You are at school.'

'My other school,' said Eileen, 'what I usually go to,

in London. Our term doesn't start till Thursday, see. I expect we broke up later than you. I come to stay with my auntie over Easter, but she went back to work yesterday, and I got bored, so I thought I'd come and see what this school was like.'

They stood in a row and gaped at her, astounded, admiring; thwarted.

'And it's all right,' Eileen assured them. 'It's all right, this school is. You can get away with murder!'